Dedicated to all
the light seekers

All rights reserved. Published in the United States by Doubleday, an imprint of
Random House Children's Books, a division of Penguin Random House LLC, New York.
Originally published in the United Kingdom by Oxford University Press, Oxford, in 2021.

Doubleday is a registered trademark and the Doubleday colophon
is a trademark of Penguin Random House LLC.

Visit us on the Web! rhcbooks.com

Educators and librarians, for a variety of teaching tools,
visit us at RHTeachersLibrarians.com

Library of Congress Cataloging-in-Publication Data
Name: Zommer, Yuval, author, illustrator.
Title: The lights that dance in the night / Yuval Zommer.
Description: First American edition. | New York : Doubleday Books for Young Readers, [2022] |
"Originally published in the United Kingdom by Oxford University Press,
Oxford, in 2021." | Audience: Ages 3–7.
Summary: From tiny specks of dust to gleaming rays in the dark, the northern lights travel
across the Arctic, creating a special magic for the animals and people living in the land below.
Identifiers: LCCN 2021044135 | ISBN 978-0-593-56313-7 (hardcover)
Subjects: CYAC: Stories in rhyme. | Auroras—Fiction. | LCGFT: Picture books. |
Stories in rhyme.
Classification: LCC PZ8.3.Z63 Li 2022 | DDC [E]—dc23

MANUFACTURED IN CHINA
10 9 8 7 6 5 4 3 2 1
First American Edition

THE LIGHTS THAT DANCE IN THE NIGHT

YUVAL ZOMMER

Doubleday Books for Young Readers

We are the lights
that dance in the night.

We started our journey as specks
of dust blown to Earth
from the sun.

We tumbled through clouds, through winds and snowstorms too.

Staying strong,
keeping together,

we found a path through
wintry weather.

And then we changed,
as in a dream.
Through streams of air
we shone. We gleamed.

We knew what we
were meant to be.

We are the lights
that dance in the night.

Our colors brought joy to polar bears
and happiness to arctic hares.

Flippers clapped to see us swirl
and bright bills touched with every twirl.

Our dancing lights made whales sing
and bells on boats began to ring.

We sashayed for an arctic fox.
We swayed above an old musk ox.

Wolf packs howled beneath our glow
and wildcats played on painted snow.

We lit the skies for forest birds.
We sparkled over reindeer herds.

Storytellers wove our lights
into tales for long, dark nights.

People stopped to stand and stare,
to feel the magic in the air.

Young and old,

big and small,

joined together, one and all.

Across this sweep of land and sea,
they raised their voices cheerfully.

Through clouds

and winds

and storms

we came . . .

. . . illuminating darkness,
keeping hope aflame.

A miracle of winter . . .
we are the lights
that dance in the night.